For: Holy Spirit Aca'

Fr Aura Guerra-Artola

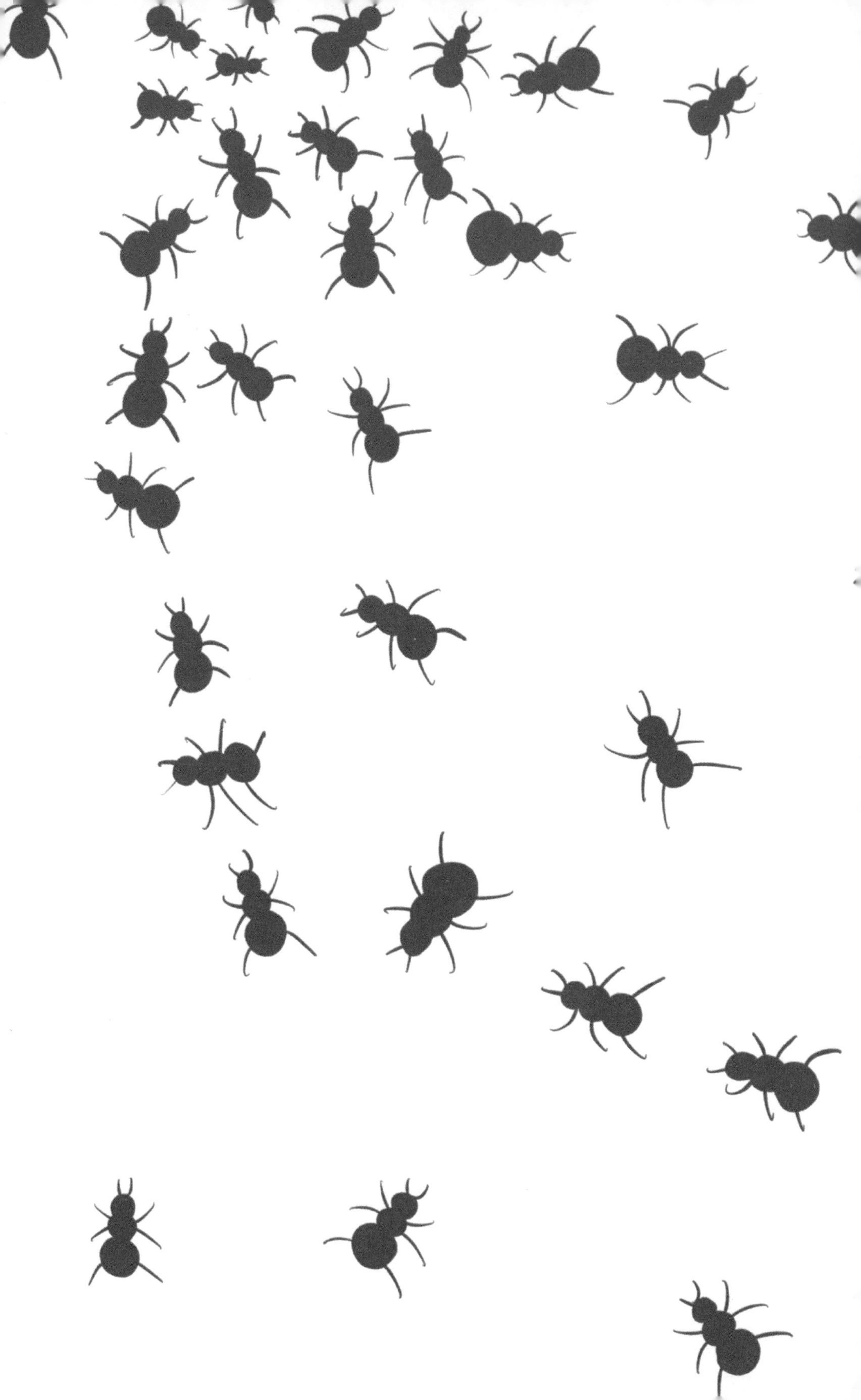

This book
belongs to: _____

ORONTES
GREAT IDEAS®

Orontes Group
www.orontesgroup.ca
Email: contact@orontesgroup.ca
Phone: +1 (587) 439-5324

Published and Distributed by Orontes Group
January 2021
1st edition

Written by Aura Guerra-Artola
Illustrated by Maria Fernandez

Copyright © 2020 by Aura Guerra-Artola

Scripture quotations are taken from the Holy Bible, New Living Translation, copyright ©1996, 2004, 2015 by Tyndale House Foundation. Used by permission of Tyndale House Publishers, a Division of Tyndale House Ministries, Carol Stream, Illinois 60188. All rights reserved.

All rights reserved. No part of this publication may be reproduced, stored in a retrieval system, or transmitted in any form or by any means, electronic, mechanical, photocopy, recording, or otherwise, without written permission of the copyright owner or publisher.

ISBN 978-1-7774905-1-5 (Printed version)
ISBN 978-1-7774905-0-8 (Digital version)

JACK'S L·I·F·E in THE BOX

To my son Chris, whose imagination made this book possible.

Aura G-A

8

Jack made a box out of cardboard and plastic. He was scared of ants, so the idea was fantastic.

He was happy to live in an insect-free world. But his friends had questions about this odd invention.

Hello, Jack! - said George.

What do you have inside that box?

I have a sandwich, a book, and a plant. I have everything except for ants!

Hey Jack! - said Dug.

Why don't you come out and play?

Outside with the bugs?
No way!

I'm hiding to keep the ants away.

Hey there, Jack! - said Jessie.

Oh boy! Your box looks messy!

Well, if I open it and clean it up, the pesky ants will get inside the box.

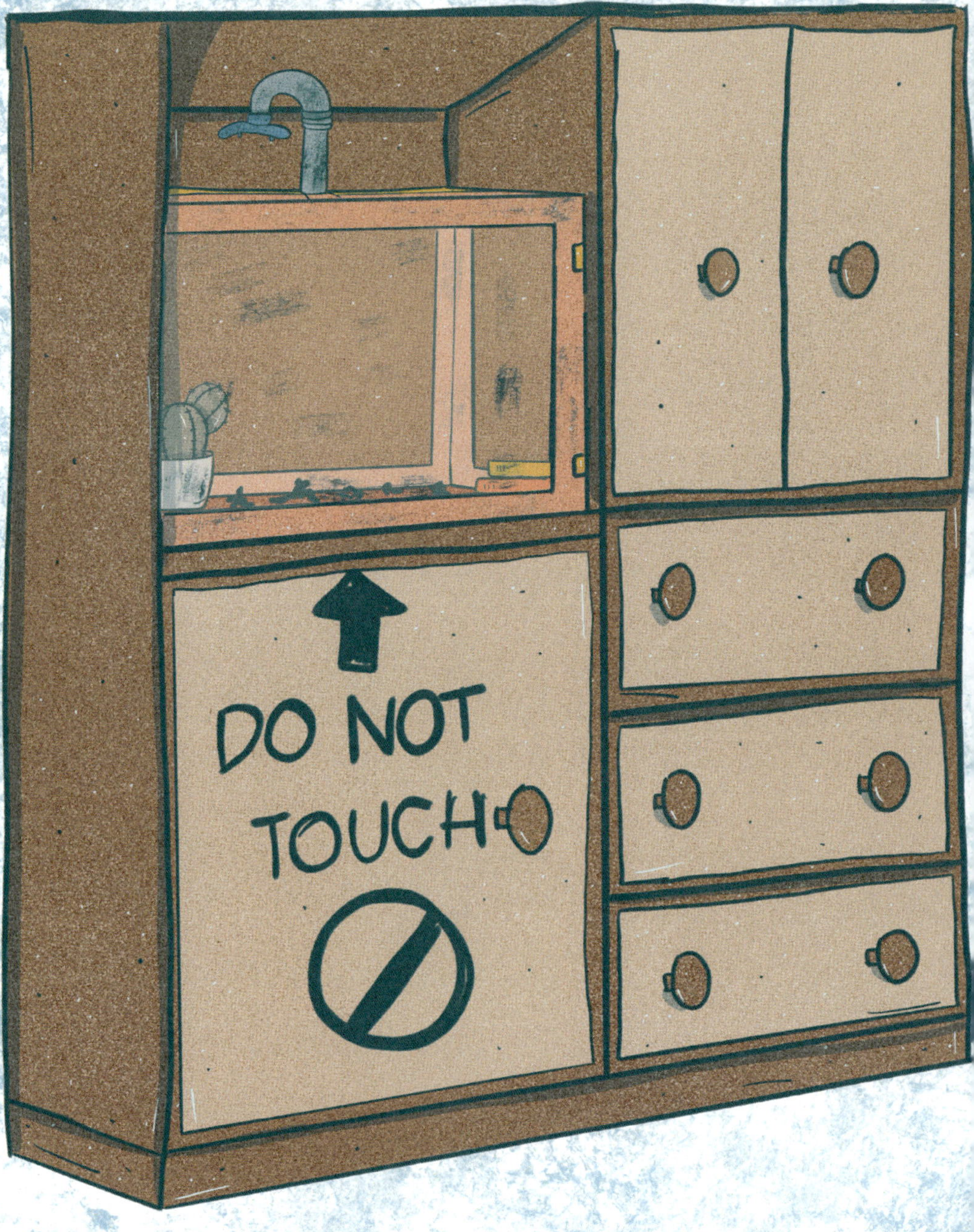
DO NOT
TOUCH

At nighttime, Jack's mom said: "Get out of that box and cleanup for bed." Jack obeyed.

He opened his closet and stored the box away.

18

It was late, Jack was fast asleep and into the room his brother sneaked.

He grabbed the box and opened it wide. He saw a candy bar and even a pumpkin pie.

20

Jack's brother ate the treats he found.

He left the box open with crumbs all around.

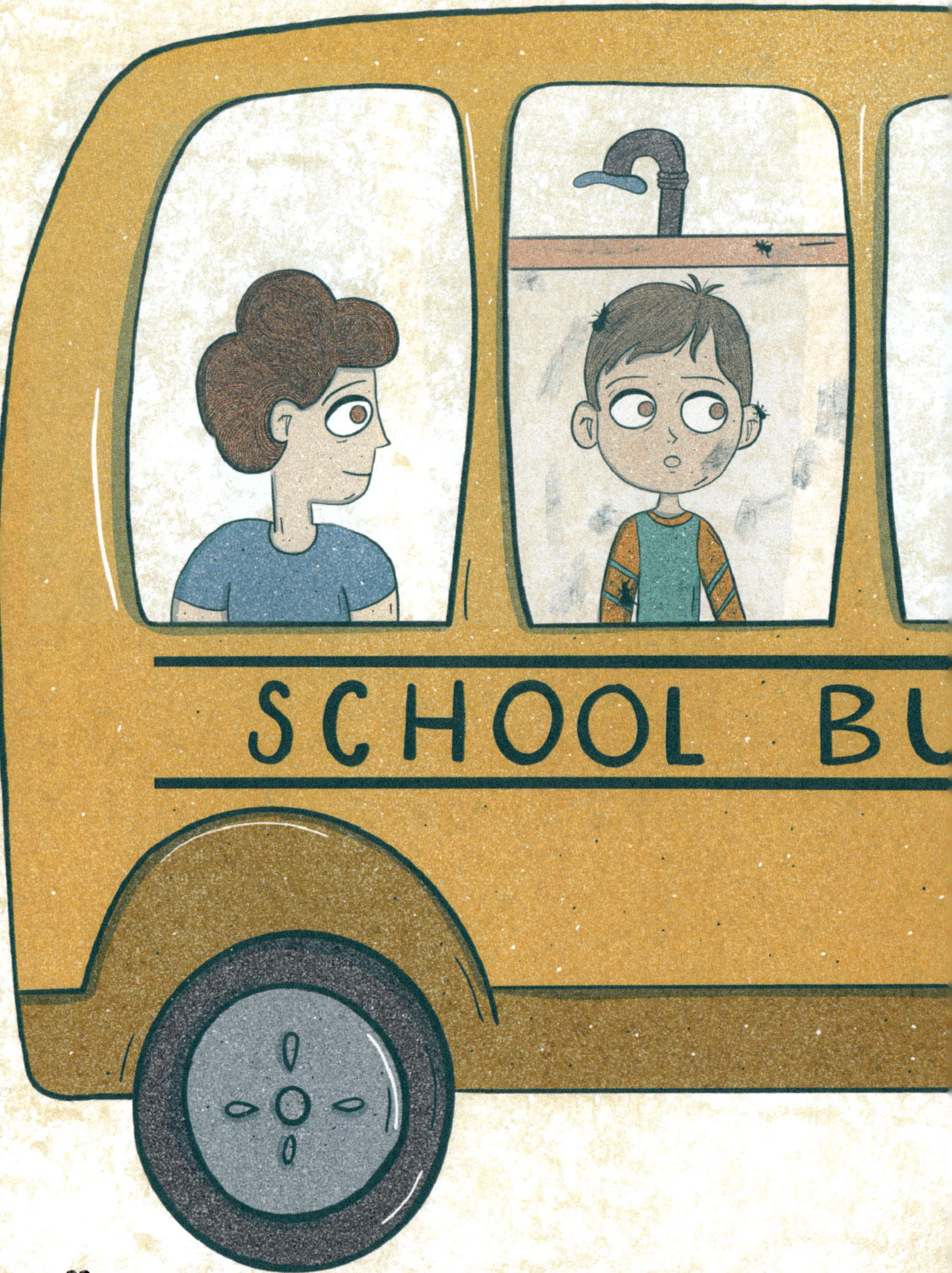
SCHOOL BU

The next day Jack rushed to catch the bus.

When he got inside his box, he felt a little tickly, and then he thought:

Could it be my allergy to fuzz?

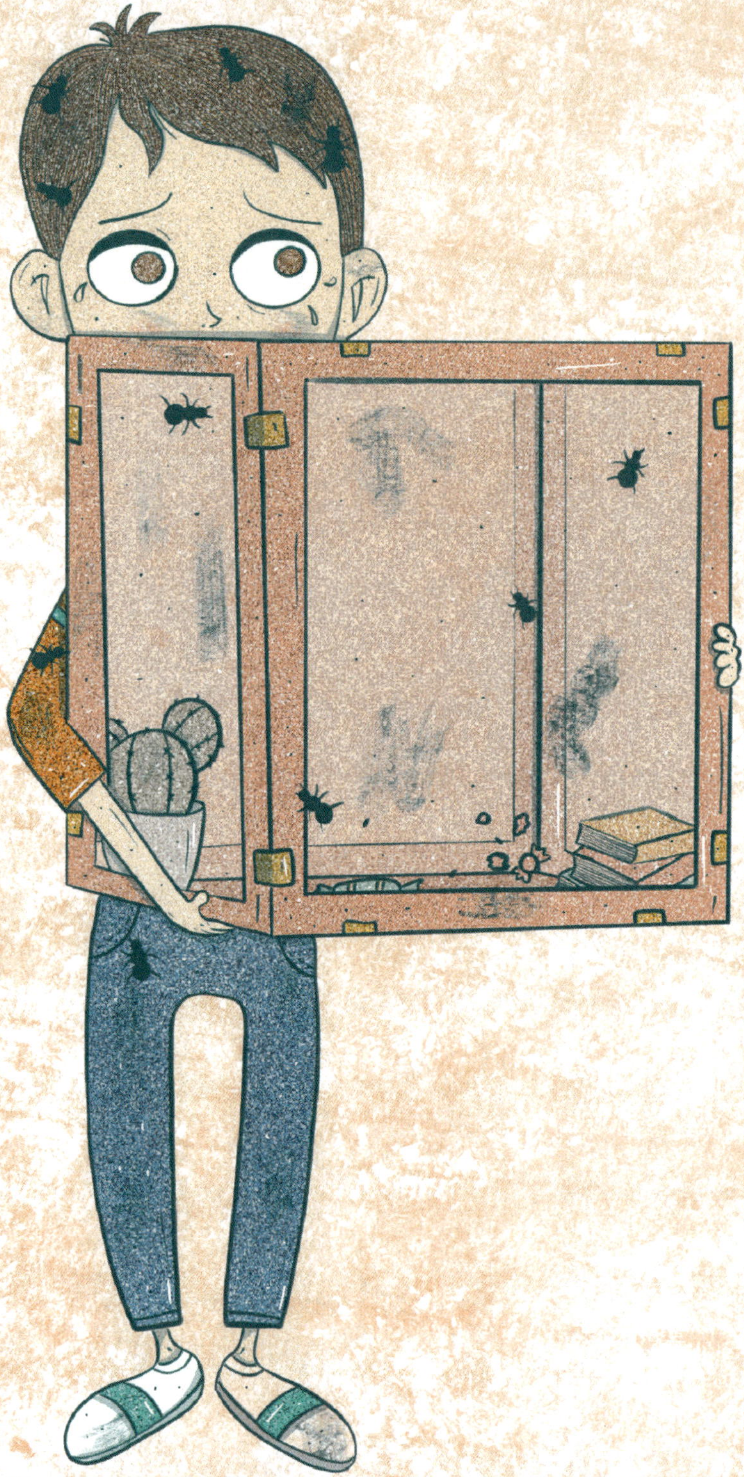

As he entered school, everyone stared. Then someone screamed:

"Jack, there are ants on your hair!"

Jack replied:

Ants, on me? No way! My ant-proof box keeps them all away.

He saw the ants and
realized it was true.

He had ants all over him,
and they were stuck
like glue.

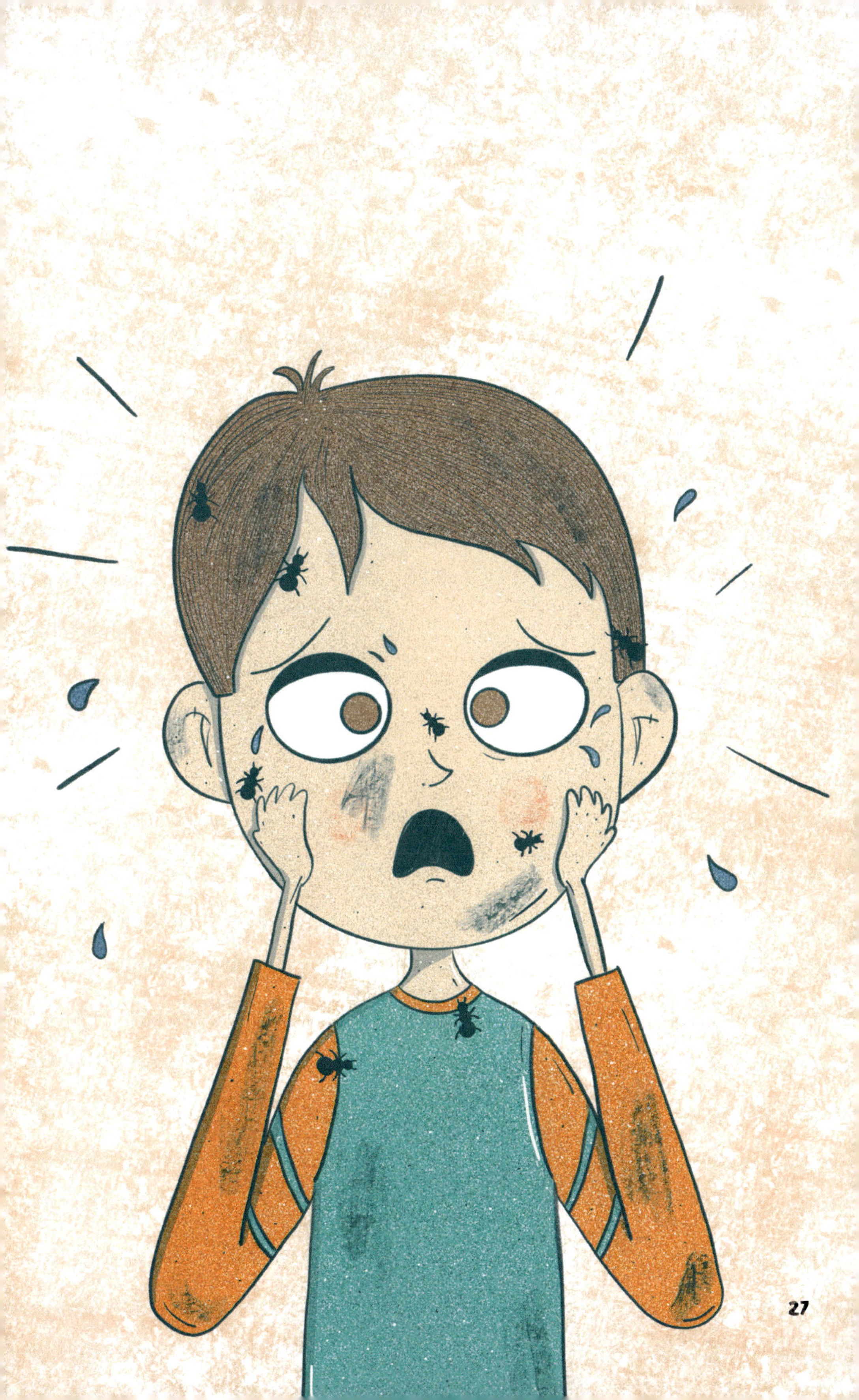

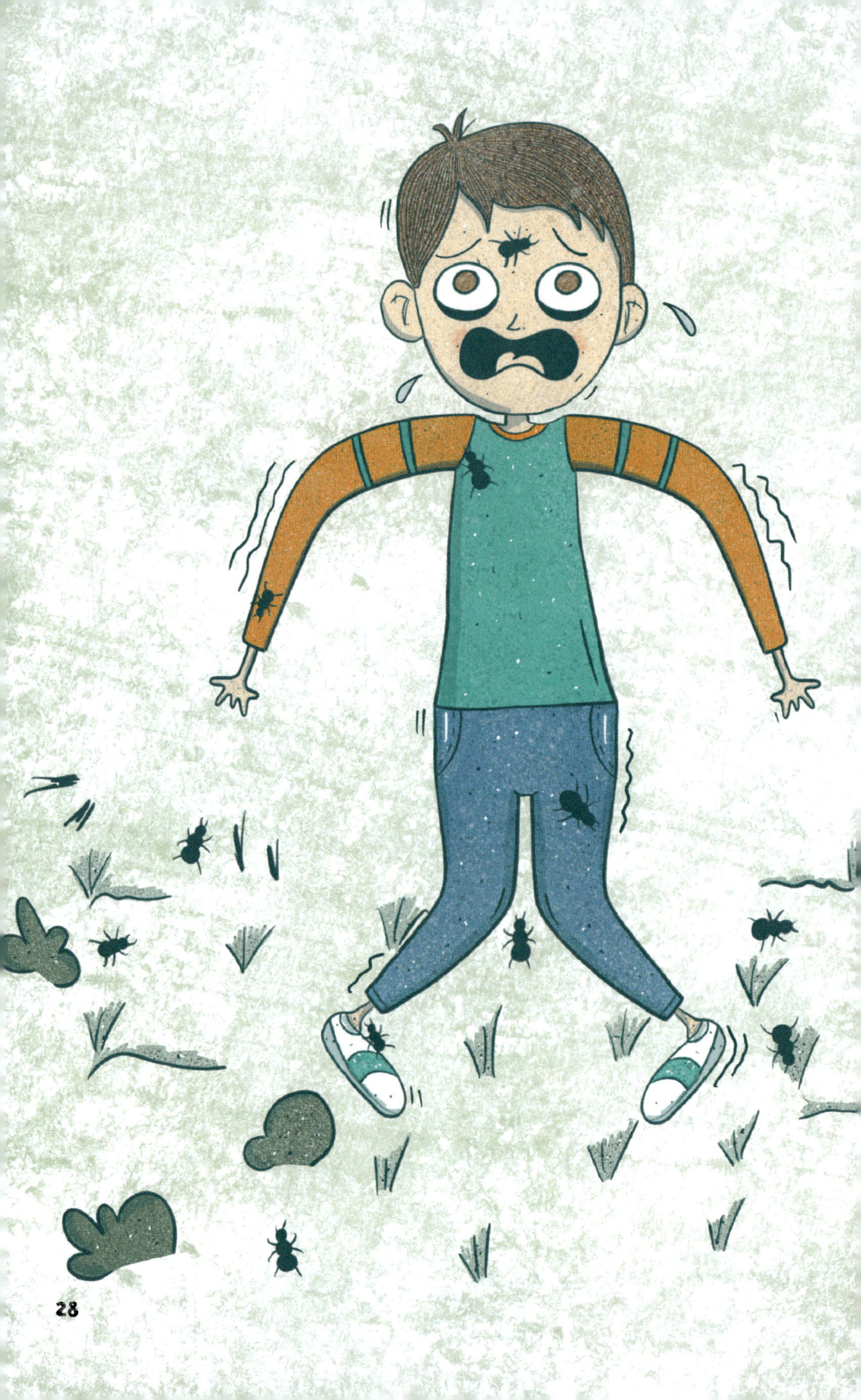

He threw away his box and wiggled around. The ants were everywhere, all over the playground.

As the ants were all gone, Jack was left alone. He was alright but didn't know what went wrong.

Jack shed some tears.
Then his teacher drew
near!

With all her knowledge, she
helped him comprehend,
that ants are harmless, and
they are nature's friends.

They just look for food
to take into their colony,
helping the earth breathe,
which is good for the
ecology.

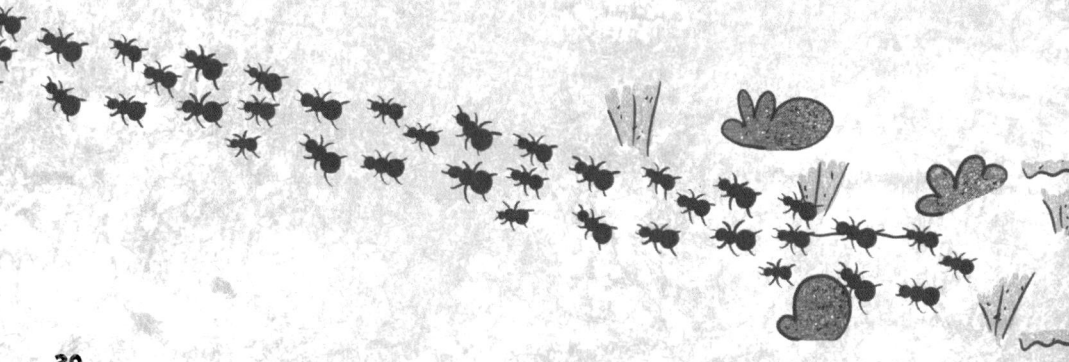

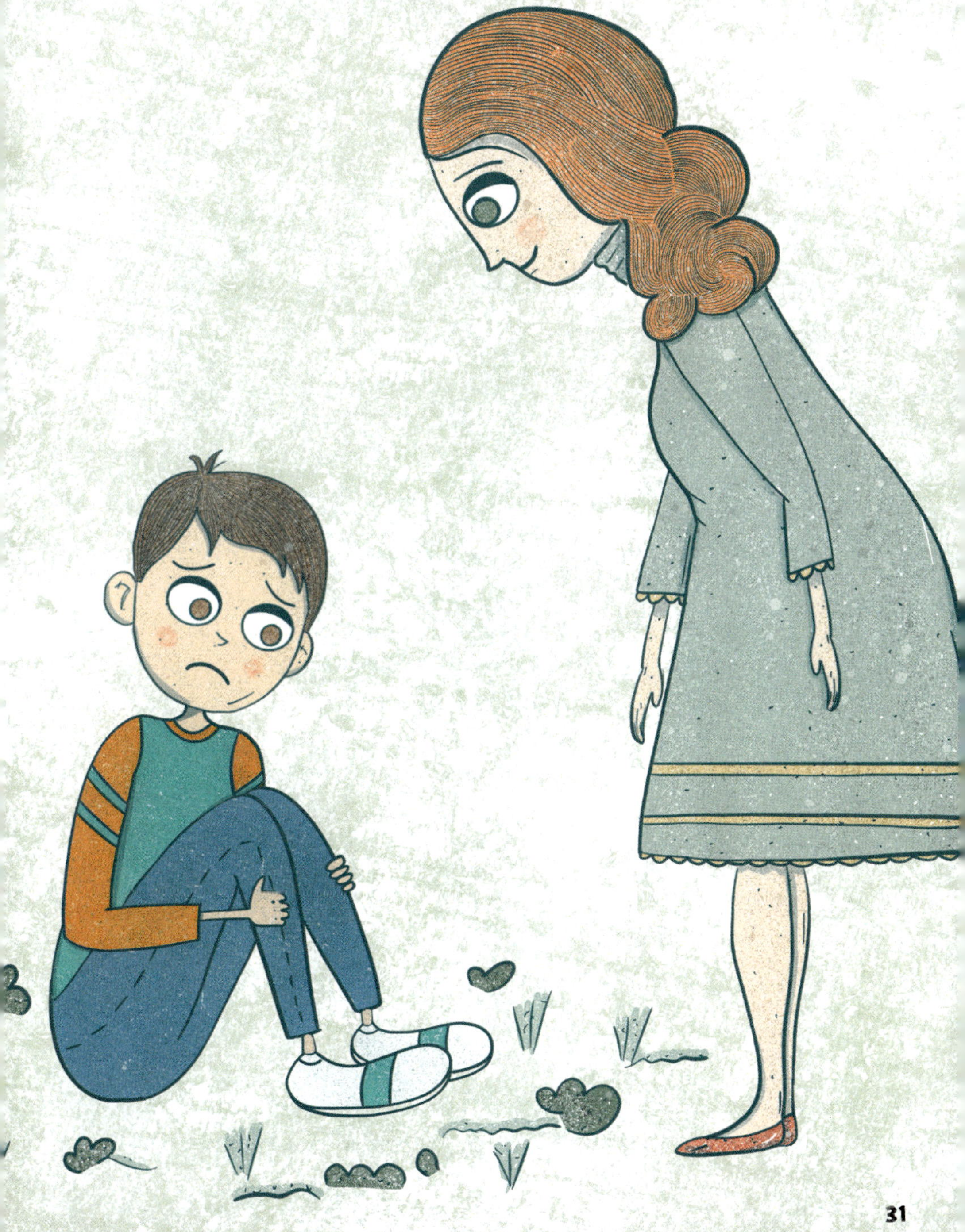

32

Jack understood that instead of hiding away, talking about his feelings is the smartest way.

Don't hide from things that make you scared. You'll be missing a beautiful world out there.

Jack was brave and chose to throw his box away. Now he was free to laugh, run, and play.

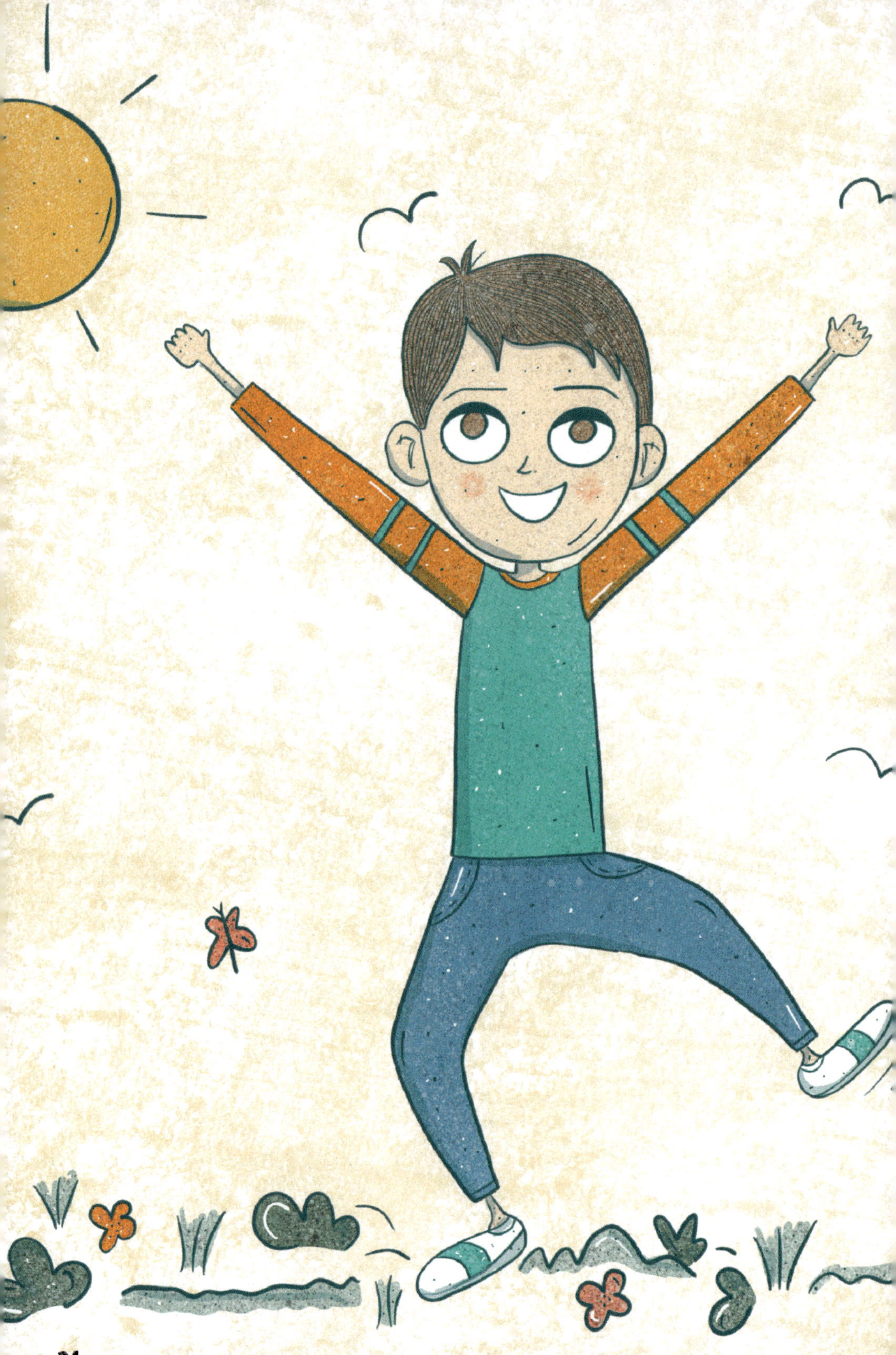

Tell a grownup or a friend. Look up things that you don't understand.

Talk to Jesus, say a prayer! He promised that all our fears, He will bear.

When Jack came out of his hiding place, he felt fantastic! He was no longer afraid. He was quite enthusiastic.

~ The End ~

I PRAYED to the LORD AND HE ANSWERED me

He FREED me from all my fears

Psalm 34:4

Verses To Ponder

I prayed to the Lord, and he answered me.
He freed me from all my fears
Psalm 34:4

For God has not given us a spirit of fear and timidity, but of power, love, and self-discipline.
2 Timothy 1:7

Then Jesus said, "Come to me, all of you who are weary and carry heavy burdens, and I will give you rest
Mathew 11:28

The Spirit of the Lord is upon me,
for he has anointed me to bring Good News to the poor.
He has sent me to proclaim that captives will be released,
that the blind will see,
that the oppressed will be set free...
Luke 4:18

Notes

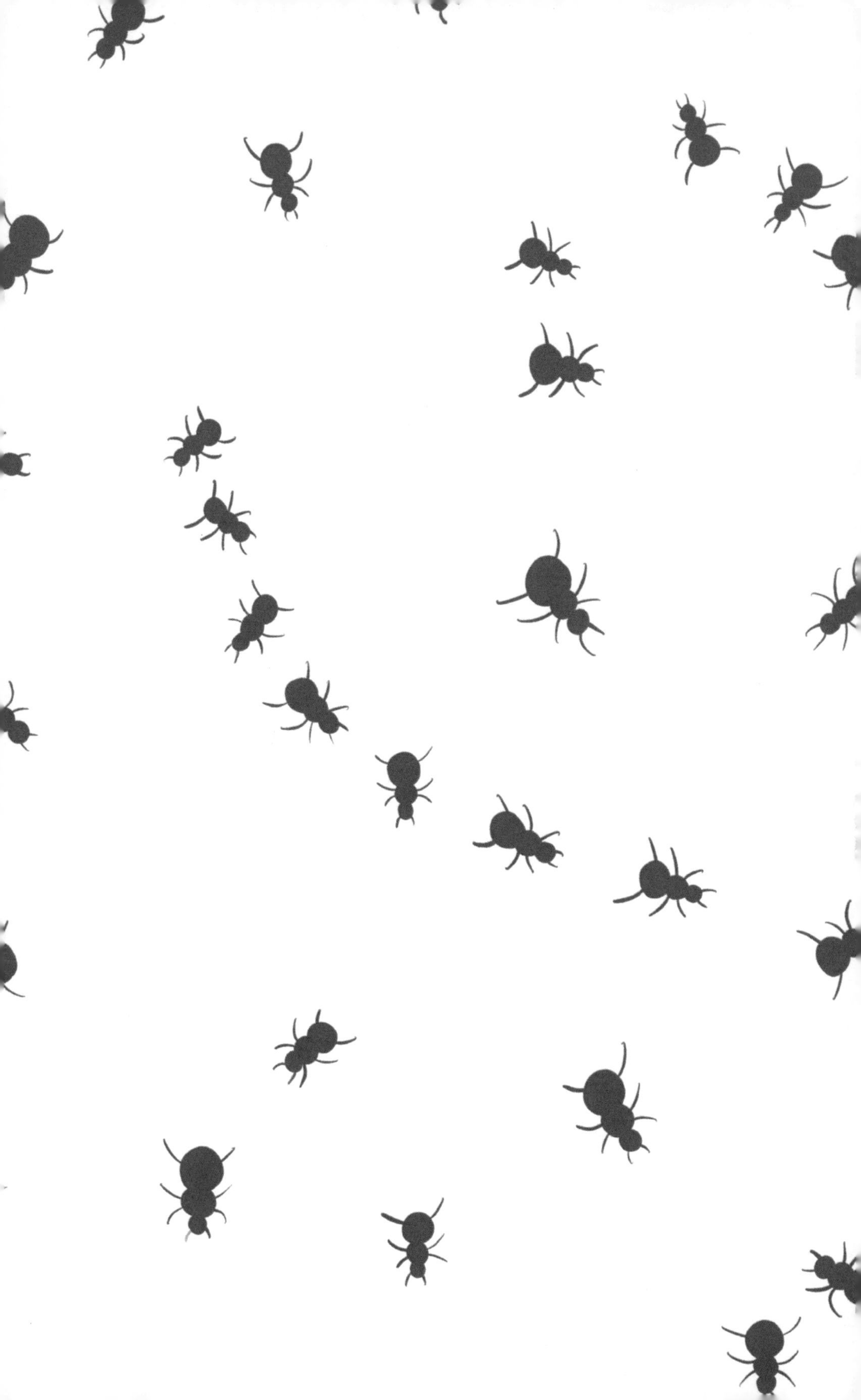

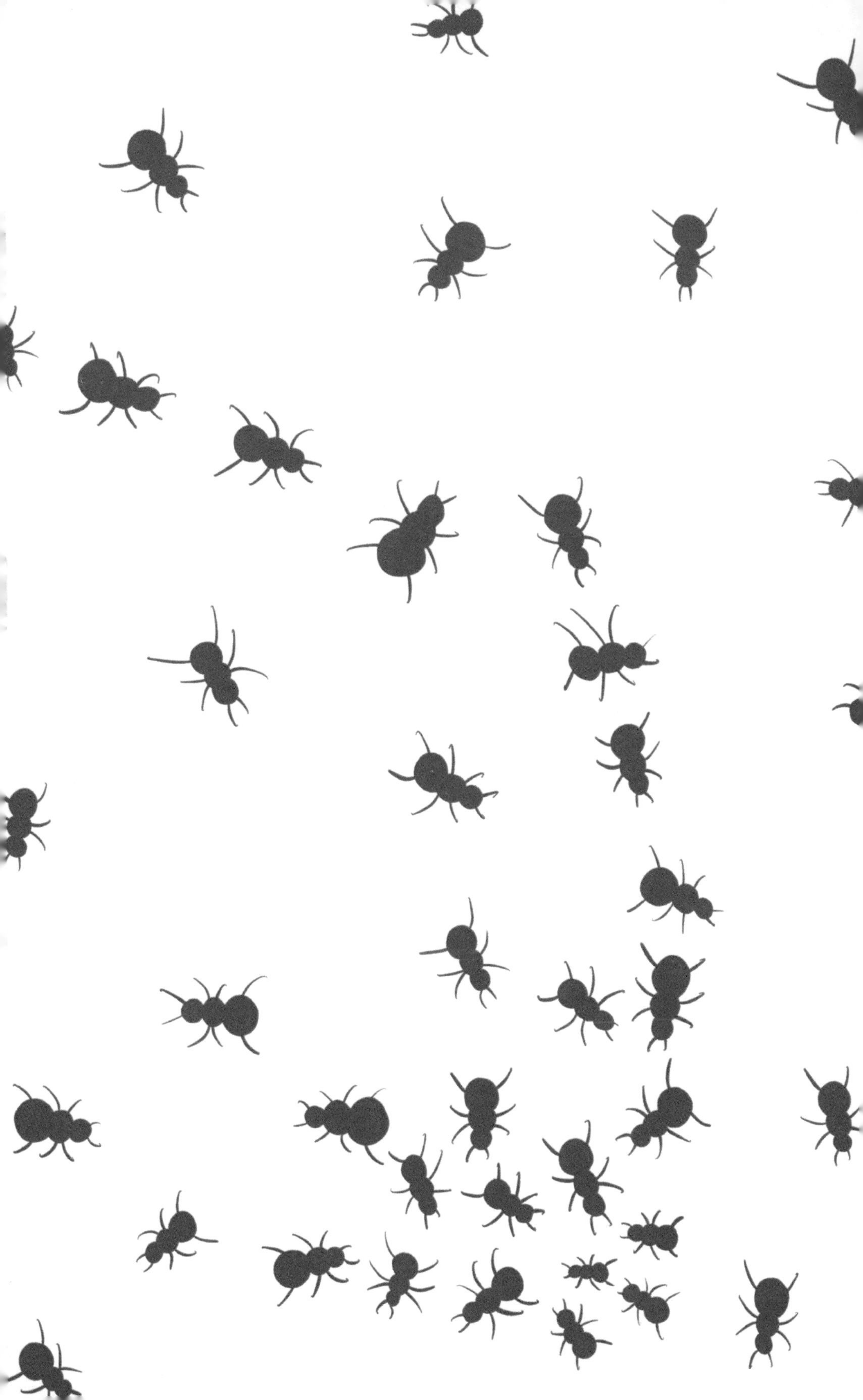

Manufactured by Amazon.ca
Bolton, ON